The Return of Toad

from
The Wind in the Willows

Written by
KENNETH GRAHAME

Abridged and illustrated by
INGA MOORE

TED SMART

The Return of Toad

The Rat put out a paw, gripped Toad by the scruff of the neck, and gave a great hoist and pull; and the waterlogged Toad came up over the edge of the hole till at last he stood in the hall, streaked with mud and weed, but happy and high-spirited, now that he found himself once more in the house of a friend.

"O Ratty!" he cried. "I've been through such times since I saw you last, you can't think! Just hold on till I tell you—"

"Toad," said the Water Rat, "go upstairs at once, and take off that old cotton rag that looks as if it belonged to some washer-woman. I'll have something to say to you later!"

Toad was at first inclined to stop and do some talking back at him. He had had enough of being ordered about in prison. However, he caught sight of himself in the looking-glass over the hatstand, with the rusty black bonnet perched rakishly over one eye, and he changed his mind and went very quickly upstairs to the Rat's dressing-room.

By the time he came down again luncheon was on the table. While they ate, Toad told the Rat all his adventures. The more he talked, the more grave and silent the Rat became.

When at last Toad had talked himself to a standstill, the Rat said, "Now, Toady, seriously, don't you see what an ass you've been making of yourself? You've been handcuffed, imprisoned, starved, chased, insulted and ignominiously flung into the water. Where's the amusement in that? Where does the fun come in? And all because you must needs go and steal a motor-car. You've never had anything but trouble from the moment you set eyes on one. Think of your friends. Do you suppose it's any pleasure to me to hear animals saying I'm the chap that keeps company with gaol-birds?"

Toad heaved a deep sigh and said, "Quite right, Ratty! I've been a conceited ass, I can see that. As for motor-cars, I've not been so keen about them since my last ducking in that river of yours. The fact is, I've had enough of adventures. I shall lead a quiet life, pottering about Toad Hall; and I shall keep a pony-chaise to jog about the country in, as I used to in the old days."

"Do you mean you haven't *heard*?" cried the Rat.

"Heard what?" said Toad, turning pale.

"About the Stoats and Weasels?"

"No!" cried Toad. "What have they been doing?"

"They've been and taken Toad Hall!"

A large tear welled up in each of Toad's eyes, overflowed and splashed on the table, plop! plop!

"When you got into that – trouble of yours," said the Rat, "it was a good deal talked about down here. Animals took sides. The River-bankers stuck up for you. But the Wild Wood animals said hard things, served you right. You were done for this time! You would never come back again, never! And one night, a band of weasels and ferrets and stoats broke into Toad Hall, and have been living there ever since!"

"O, have they!" said Toad, getting up and seizing a stick. "I'll jolly soon see about that!"

"It's no good!" called the Rat after him. "You'll only get into trouble."

But there was no holding the Toad. He marched down the road, his stick over his shoulder, till he got near his front gate, when suddenly there popped up from behind the palings a long yellow ferret with a gun.

"Who comes there?" said the ferret sharply.

"What do you mean by talking like that to me?" said Toad very angrily. "Come out or I'll—"

The ferret said never a word, but brought his gun to his shoulder. Toad dropped flat in the road and *Bang!* a bullet whistled over his head.

The startled Toad scrambled to his feet and scampered down the road; and as he ran he heard the ferret laughing a horrid, thin little laugh.

He went back, got out the boat, and set off rowing up river to where the garden of Toad Hall came down to the waterside.

Arriving within sight of his old home, he rested on his oars

and surveyed the land cautiously.

All seemed very peaceful and deserted. He would try the boat-house first, he thought. Very warily he paddled up the creek, and was just passing under the bridge, when ... *Crash!*

A great stone, dropped from above, smashed through the bottom of the boat. It filled and sank, and Toad found himself struggling in deep water. Looking up, he saw two stoats leaning over the parapet of the bridge, watching him with glee. "It will be your head next time, Toady!" they called out to him. Toad swam to shore while the stoats laughed and laughed.

"Well, *what* did I tell you?" said the Rat crossly, when Toad related his disappointing experiences. "And now you've been and lost me my boat! And simply ruined that nice suit I lent you! Really, Toad, be patient. We can do nothing until we have seen the Mole and the Badger."

"O, ah, yes, the Mole and the Badger," said Toad. "What's become of the dear fellows? I had forgotten all about them."

"Well may you ask!" said the Rat reproachfully. "While you were riding about in motor-cars, and breakfasting on the fat of the land, those two animals have been camping out in every sort of weather, watching over your house, contriving how to get it back for you. You don't deserve such loyal friends, Toad, you don't, really."

"I know," sobbed Toad. "Let me go and find them, and share their hardships, and— Hold on! Supper's here, hooray!"

They had just finished their meal when there came a heavy knock at the door, and in walked Mr Badger. His shoes were covered with mud, and he was looking rough and tousled; but then he had never been very smart, Badger. He came solemnly up to Toad, shook him by the paw, and said, "Welcome home, Toad!" Then he helped himself to a large slice of cold pie.

Presently there came another, lighter knock and the Rat ushered in the Mole, very shabby and unwashed, with bits of hay and straw sticking in his fur.

"Toad!" cried the Mole, beaming. "Fancy having you back! We never dreamt you would turn up so soon! Why, you must have managed to escape, you clever Toad!"

The Rat pulled him by the elbow; but it was too late.

"Clever? O no!" said Toad. "Not according to my friends. I've only broken out of the strongest prison in England, that's all! And captured a railway train and escaped on it, that's all! And disguised myself and gone about the country humbugging everybody, that's all! O no! I'm a stupid ass, I am!"

He straddled the hearth-rug, thrust his paw into his pocket and pulled out a handful of silver. "Look at that!" he cried, displaying it. "Not bad for a few minutes' work! And how do you think I done it, Mole? Horse-dealing! That's how!"

"Toad, be quiet!" said the Rat. "And don't you egg him on, Mole, when you know what he is; tell us what the position is, now Toad is back at last."

"About as bad as it can be," replied the Mole. "Badger and I have been round and round the place; always the same thing. Sentries posted everywhere, guns poked out at us, always an animal on the look-out, and when they see us, my! how they laugh! That's what annoys me most!"

The Badger, having finished his pie, got up from his seat and stood before the fireplace.

"Toad!" he said severely. "You bad little animal! Aren't you ashamed of yourself? Think what your father would have said if he had been here tonight, and known of all your goings-on! What Mole says is true. The stoats are on guard, at every point. It's quite useless to think of attacking the place."

"Then it's all over," sobbed the Toad. "I shall go and enlist for a soldier, and never see my dear Toad Hall any more!"

"Cheer up, Toady!" said the Badger. "There are more ways of getting back a place than taking it by storm. I haven't said my last word yet. Now I'm going to tell you a secret."

Toad dried his eyes. Secrets had an immense attraction for him, because he never could keep one.

"There – is – an – underground – passage," said the Badger impressively, "that leads from the river bank quite near here, right up into the middle of Toad Hall."

"Nonsense! Badger," said Toad airily. "You've been listening to some of the yarns they spin in the public-houses about here. I know every inch of Toad Hall, inside and out. Nothing of the sort, I do assure you!"

"My young friend," said the Badger with severity, "your father, who was a worthy animal – a lot worthier than some I know – was a particular friend of mine, and told me a great deal he wouldn't have dreamt of telling you. He discovered that passage – of course it was made hundreds of years before he ever came to live there – and he repaired it and cleaned it out, because he thought it might come in useful some day, in case of trouble or danger, and he showed it to me. 'Don't let my son know about it,' he said. 'He's a good boy, but simply cannot hold his tongue. If he's ever in a real fix, and it would be of use to him, you may tell him about the secret passage; but not before.'"

The other animals looked to see how Toad would take it.

"Well," he said, "perhaps I am a bit of a talker. A popular fellow such as I am – my friends get round me – and somehow my tongue gets wagging. I have the gift of conversation. I've been told I ought to have a *salon*, whatever that may be. Go on, Badger. How's this passage of yours going to help us?"

"I've found out a thing or two lately," continued the Badger. "There's going to be a big banquet tomorrow night. It's somebody's birthday – the Chief Weasel's, I believe – and all the weasels will be gathered in the dining-hall, eating and drinking and carrying on, suspecting nothing. No guns, no swords, no sticks, no arms of any sort whatever!"

"But the sentinels will be posted as usual," remarked the Rat.

"Exactly," said the Badger; "that is my point. The weasels will trust entirely to their sentinels. That is where the passage comes in. That useful tunnel leads right up under the butler's pantry, next to the dining-hall!"

"Aha! that squeaky board in the butler's pantry!" said Toad. "Now I understand it!"

"We shall creep out into the pantry—" cried the Mole.

"—with our pistols, swords and sticks—" shouted the Rat.

"— and rush in upon them," said the Badger.

"— and whack 'em,"

"and whack 'em,"

"and whack 'em!" cried the Toad in ecstasy, running round and round the room.

"Very well, then," said the Badger, "our plan is settled and there's nothing more to argue about. So, as it's getting late, all of you go off to bed at once. We will make the necessary arrangements in the morning."

Toad slept late next morning, and by the time he got down, found the other animals had finished their breakfast some time before. The Mole had slipped off by himself, without telling anyone where he was going. The Badger sat in the armchair, reading the paper, and the Rat was running round the room busily, distributing weapons in four little heaps on the floor.

Presently the Mole came tumbling into the room, evidently pleased with himself. "I've been having such fun!" he began; "I've been getting a rise out of the stoats!"

"I hope you've been careful, Mole?" said the Rat.

"I hope so, too," said the Mole. "I got the idea when I found Toad's old washerwoman-dress hanging in the kitchen. I put it on, and off I went to Toad Hall, as bold as you please. 'Good morning, gentlemen!' says I. 'Want any washing done today?'

"They looked at me very proud and stiff and haughty, and said, 'Go away, washerwoman! We don't do washing on duty.' 'Or any other time?' says I. Ho, ho, ho! Some of the stoats turned quite pink, and the sergeant said, 'Run away, my good woman!' 'Run away?' says I; 'it won't be me running away, in a very short time from now!'"

"O, *Moly*, how could you?" said the Rat, dismayed.

The Badger laid down his paper.

"I could see them pricking up their ears and looking at each other," went on the Mole; "and the sergeant said to them, 'Never mind *her*; she doesn't know what she's talking about.'

"'O! don't I?' said I. 'Well, my daughter washes for Mr Badger, and that'll show you whether I know! A hundred bloodthirsty Badgers are going to attack Toad Hall this very night, by way of the paddock. Six boat-loads of rats will come up the river while a picked body of toads, known as the Die-hards, or the Death-or-Glory Toads, will storm the orchard and carry every-thing before them. There won't be much left of you to wash, by the time they've done with you.' Then I ran away and hid;

and presently I came creeping back along the ditch and took a peep at them through the hedge. They were all as nervous as could be, running all ways at once, and I heard them saying 'That's *just* like the weasels; they're to stop comfortably in the banqueting-hall, and have feasting and songs and all sorts of fun, while we must stay on guard in the cold and dark, and be cut to pieces by bloodthirsty Badgers!'"

"You silly ass, Mole!" cried Toad. "You've been and spoilt everything!"

"Mole," said the Badger. "You have managed excellently. I begin to have great hopes of you. Clever Mole!"

The Toad was wild with jealousy, especially as he couldn't make out for the life of him what the Mole had done that was so clever; fortunately for him, before he could show temper, the bell rang for luncheon.

It was a simple but sustaining meal – bacon and broad beans, and a macaroni pudding; and when they had done, the Badger settled himself into an arm-chair, and said, "I'm just going to take forty winks, while I can." And he was soon snoring. The anxious Rat resumed his preparations, running between his heaps. So the Mole drew his arm through Toad's, led him into the open air, shoved him into a wicker chair, and made him tell all his adventures from beginning to end. Toad rather let himself go. Indeed, much he related belonged more to the category of what-might-have-happened-had-I-only-thought-of-it-in-time-instead-of-ten-minutes-afterwards. Those are always the best and the raciest adventures; and why should they not be ours, as much as the things that really come off?

When it began to grow dark, the Rat summoned them back into the parlour, stood each of them alongside his little heap, and proceeded to dress them up for the coming expedition. First, there was a belt to go round each animal, then a sword to be stuck into each belt, and then a cutlass on the other side to balance it. Then a pair of pistols, a policeman's truncheon, several sets of handcuffs, some bandages and sticking-plaster, and a flask and a sandwich-case. The Badger laughed and said, "I'm going to do all I've got to do with this here stick." But the Rat only said, "*Please*, Badger! You know I shouldn't like you to say I had forgotten *anything*!"

When all was quite ready, the Badger took a lantern in one paw, grasped his great stick with the other, and said, "Now then, follow me!"

The Badger led the animals along by the river for a little way, and then into a hole in the bank. At last they were in the secret passage, and the expedition had begun! It was low and narrow, and Toad began to shiver from dread of what might be before him. The lantern was far ahead, and he could not help lagging behind in the darkness. He heard the Rat call out "*Come* on, Toad!" and a terror seized him of being left alone, and he "came on" with such a rush that he upset the Rat into the Mole and the Mole into the Badger, and all was confusion. They groped and shuffled along, with their ears pricked up and their paws on their pistols, till at last the Badger said, "We ought to be nearly under the Hall."

Then suddenly they heard, far away as it might be, and yet nearly over their heads, shouting and cheering and stamping on the floor. Toad's terrors all returned, but the Badger only remarked, "They *are* going it, the weasels!"

The passage now began to slope upwards; and the noise broke out again, quite distinct this time, and very close above them. "Ooo-ray-oo-ray-oo-ray-ooray!" they heard, and the stamping of feet on the floor, and clinking of glasses as fists pounded on the table. "Come on!" said Badger. They hurried along till the passage came to a full stop, and they found themselves standing under the trap-door that led up into the butler's pantry.

The Badger said, "Now, boys, all together!" and they heaved the trap-door back.

The noise, as they emerged, was simply deafening. As the cheering and hammering slowly subsided, a voice could be made out saying, "Before I resume my seat I should like to say one word about our kind host, Mr Toad. We all know Toad! *Good* Toad, *modest* Toad, *honest* Toad!"

"Let me get at him!" muttered Toad, grinding his teeth.

"Hold hard a minute!" said the Badger, restraining him with difficulty. "Get ready, all of you!"

"Let me sing you a song," went on the voice, "which I have composed on the subject of Toad −" Then the Chief Weasel − for it was he − began in a high, squeaky voice:

> *Toad he went a-pleasuring*
> *Gaily down the street −*

The Badger drew himself up, took a firm grip of his stick, and cried: "Follow me!" And flung the door open.

My! What a squealing and squeaking filled the air!
Well might the weasels spring at the windows!
Well might the ferrets rush for the chimney!
Well might tables and chairs be upset,
and glass and china be sent crashing
on the floor, in the panic of that
terrible moment when the four
Heroes strode into the room!
The mighty Badger, his whiskers
bristling, his great cudgel whistling
through the air; Mole, black and grim,
brandishing his stick, shouting his
awful war-cry, "A Mole! A Mole!"
Rat, desperate and determined, his
belt bulging with weapons of every
age and variety; Toad, swollen to
twice his ordinary size, emitting
Toad-whoops that chilled them
to the marrow! "Toad he went
a-pleasuring!" he yelled.
"I'll pleasure 'em!" and
he went straight for
the Chief Weasel.

Up and down strode the four Friends, whacking every head that showed itself; and in five minutes the room was cleared. Through the broken windows the shrieks of escaping weasels were borne faintly to their ears; on the floor lay some dozen or so of the enemy, on whom the Mole was busily engaged in fitting handcuffs. The Badger wiped his brow.

"Mole," he said, "you're the best of fellows! Just cut along outside, and see what those sentries are doing. I've an idea, thanks to you, we shan't have much trouble from *them*!"

Then he said in that rather common way he had of speaking, "Stir your stumps, Toad! We've got your house back for you, and you don't offer us so much as a sandwich."

Toad felt hurt that the Badger didn't say pleasant things to him, as he had to the Mole, and tell him what a fine fellow he was, and how splendidly he had fought; for he was rather pleased with himself and the way he had sent the Chief Weasel flying across the table. But he bustled about, and so did the Rat, and soon they found some guava jelly in a glass dish, and a cold chicken, some trifle, and quite a lot of lobster salad; and in the pantry they came upon a basket of French rolls and any quantity of cheese, butter, and celery. They were just about to sit down when the Mole clambered in through the window, chuckling, with an armful of rifles.

"It's all over," he reported. "From what I can make out, as soon as the stoats, who were very nervous and jumpy already, heard the shrieks inside the hall, they threw down their rifles and fled. So *that's* all right!"

Then Toad, like the gentleman he was, put all jealousy from him and said, "Thank you, Mole, for your trouble tonight and especially for your cleverness this morning!" So they finished their supper in great joy and contentment, safe in Toad's ancestral home; won back by matchless valour, consummate strategy, and a proper handling of sticks.

After this climax, the four animals continued to lead their lives, undisturbed by further invasions.

Sometimes, in the long summer evenings, the friends would take a stroll together in the Wild Wood, now tamed so far as they were concerned; and it was pleasing to see how respectfully they were greeted by the inhabitants; mother-weasels would bring their young ones to the mouths of their holes, and say, pointing, "Look! There goes the great Mr Toad! And that's the Water Rat, a terrible fighter. And yonder comes the famous Mr Mole, of whom you've heard your father tell!" But when their infants were fractious and quite beyond control, they would quiet them by telling how, if they didn't hush, the terrible grey Badger would up and get them. This was a base libel on Badger, who, though he cared little about Society, was rather fond of children; but it never failed to have its full effect.